S H A M E

A FROZEN WOMAN

"There are plenty of women readers for whom its bitter, sad, intelligent story of enclosure will ring true... at once private and exemplary."—Hermoine Lee in *The New York Times Book Review*

"Ernaux acutely portrays the women in her heroine's life... [in] this outstanding book."
—*Library Journal* (starred review)

EXTERIORS

"What's especially impressive about *Exteriors* is Ernaux' ability to play objectivity and engagement off each other, to revel in serendipity while providing enough epiphanies to give her investigations shape."—David Ulin in *Newsday*

"A slim, deceptively slight paste-up of daily encounters that refreshingly revives the O'Hara tradition."
—Joe Knowles in *The Nation*

"Honest, genuine and skillfully executed."
—*The Columbus Dispatch*

"I REMAIN IN DARKNESS"

"A quietly searing account."—*Publishers Weekly*

SHAME

ANNIE ERNAUX

Translated by

TANYA LESLIE

SEVEN STORIES PRESS
New York

Library of Congress Cataloging- in- Publication Data
Ernaux, Annie, 1940-
[Honte. English.
Shame / by Annie Ernaux;
translated from the French by Tanya Leslie.
p. cm.
ISBN 978-1-888363-69-2 (hc); ISBN 978-1-64421-356-8 (pbk).
Ernaux, Annie, 1940-   —Childhood and youth.
2. Authors, French—20th century—Biography.
I. Leslie, Tanya. II. Title.
PQ2665.R67Z46513   1998
843'.914—dc21   97-50426
CIP

Book design by Cindy LaBreacht
Printed in India.

9 8 7 6 5 4 3 2

À Philippe V

Language is not truth.
It is the way we exist in
the world.

Paul Auster
The Invention of Solitude

My father tried to kill my mother one Sunday in June, in the early afternoon. I had been to Mass at a quarter to twelve as usual. I must have brought back some cakes from the baker in the new shopping precinct—a cluster of temporary buildings erected after the war while reconstruction was under way. When I got home, I took off my Sunday clothes and slipped on a dress that washed easily. After the customers had left and the shutters had been pinned down over the store window, we had lunch, probably with the radio on, because at that hour there was a funny program called *Courtroom,* in which Yves Deniaud played some wretched subordinate continually charged with the most preposterous offenses and condemned to ridiculous sentences by a judge with a quavering voice. My mother was in a bad temper. The argument she started with my father as soon as she sat down lasted throughout the meal. After the table was cleared and the oilcloth wiped clean, she continued to fire criticism at my father, turning round and round in the tiny kitchen—squeezed in between the café, the store and the steps leading upstairs—as she always did when she was upset. My father was still seated at the table, saying nothing, his head turned toward the window. Suddenly he began to wheeze and was seized with convulsive shaking. He stood up and I saw him grab hold of my mother and drag her through the café, shouting in a hoarse, unfamiliar voice. I rushed upstairs and threw myself on to the bed, my face buried in a cushion. Then I heard my mother scream: "My daughter!" Her voice came from the cellar adjoining the café. I rushed downstairs, shouting "Help!" as loud as I could. In the poorly-lit cellar, my father had grabbed my mother by the shoulders, or maybe the neck. In his other hand, he was holding the scythe for cutting firewood which he had wrenched away from the block where it belonged. At this point all I can remember are sobs and screams. Then the three of us are back in the kitchen again. My father is sitting by the window, my mother is standing near the cooker and I am crouching at the foot of the stairs. I can't stop crying. My father wasn't his normal self; his hands were still trembling and he had that unfamiliar voice. He kept on repeating, "Why are you crying? I didn't do anything to you." I can recall saying this sentence, "You'll breathe disaster on me." My mother was saying, "Come on, it's over."

Afterward the three of us went for a bicycle ride in the countryside nearby. When they got back, my parents opened the café like they did every Sunday evening. That was the end of it.

It was June 15, 1952. The first date I remember with unerring accuracy from my childhood. Before that, the days and dates inscribed on the blackboard and in my copybooks seemed just to drift by.

Later on, I would say to certain men: "My father tried to kill my mother just before I turned twelve." The fact that I wanted to tell them this meant that I was crazy about them. All were quiet after hearing the sentence. I realized that I had made a mistake, that they were not able to accept such a thing.

This is the first time I am writing about what happened. Until now, I have found it impossible to do so, even in my diary. I considered writing about it to be a forbidden act that would call for punishment. Not being able to write anything else afterward, for instance. (I felt quite relieved just now when I saw that I could go on writing, that nothing terrible had happened.) In fact, now that I have finally committed it to paper, I feel that it is an ordinary incident, far more common among families than I had originally thought. It may be that narrative, any kind of narrative, lends normality to people's deeds, including the most dramatic ones. But because this scene has remained frozen inside me, an image empty of speech—except for the sentence I told my lovers—the words which I have used to describe it seem strange, almost incongruous. It has become a scene destined for other people.

Before starting, I reckoned I would be able to recall every single detail. It turns out I can remember only the general atmosphere, our respective places in the kitchen and a few words or expressions. I've forgotten how the argument actually started, what we had to eat and whether my mother was still wearing her white storekeeper's coat or whether she had taken it off in view of the bicycle ride. I have no particular memory of that Sunday morning besides the usual routine—attending Mass, buying the cakes and so on—although I have often had to think back to the time before it happened, as I would do later on for other events in my life. Yet I am sure I was wearing my blue dress, the one with white spots, because during the two summers that followed, every time I put it on, I would think, "it's the dress I wore that day." Of the weather too I am quite sure—a combination of sun, clouds and wind.

From then on, that Sunday was like a veil that came between me and everything I did. I would play, I would read, I would behave normally but somehow I wasn't there. Everything had become artificial. I had trouble learning my lessons, when before I only needed to read them once to know them by heart. Acutely aware of everything around me and yet unable to concentrate, I lost my insouciance and natural ability to learn.

What had happened was not something that could be judged. My father, who loved me, had tried to kill my mother, who also loved me. Because my mother was more religious than my father and because she did the accounts and spoke to my schoolmistresses, I suppose I thought it normal for her to shout at him the same way she shouted at me. It was no one's fault, no one was to blame. I just had to stop my father from killing my mother and going to jail.

I believe that for months, maybe even years, I waited for the scene to be repeated. I was positive it would happen again. I found the presence of customers comforting, dreading the moments when my parents and I were alone, in the evening and on Sunday afternoons. I was on the alert as soon as they raised their voices; I would scrutinize my father, his expression, his hands. In every sudden silence I would read the omens of disaster. Every day at school I wondered whether, on returning home, I would be faced with the aftermath of a tragedy.

When they did show signs of affection for each other—joking, sharing a laugh or a smile—I imagined I had gone back to the time before that day. It was just a "bad dream." One hour later I realized that these signs only meant something at the time; they offered no guarantee for the future.

Around that time a strange song was often heard on the radio, mimicking a fight that suddenly breaks out in a saloon: there was a pause, a voice whispered, "you could have heard a pin drop," followed by a cacophony of shouts and jumbled sentences. Every time I heard it I was seized with panic. One day my uncle handed me the detective story he was reading: "What would you do if your father was accused of murder but wasn't guilty?" The question sent a chill down my spine. I kept seeing the images of a tragedy which had never occurred.

The scene never did happen again. My father died fifteen years later, also on a Sunday in June.

It is only now that a thought occurs to me: my parents may have discussed both that Sunday afternoon and my father's murderous gesture; they may have arrived at an explanation or even an excuse and decided to forget the whole thing. Maybe one night after making love. This thought, like all those that elude one at the time, comes too late. It can be of no help to me now; its absence only serves to measure the indescribable terror which that Sunday has always meant to me.

In August an English family pitched their tent by the side of a small country road in the south of France. In the morning they were found murdered: the father, Sir Jack Drummond, his wife, Lady Anne, and their daughter Elizabeth. The nearest farmhouse belonged to the Dominici, a family of Italian extraction, whose son Gustave was originally accused of the three deaths. The Dominici spoke very little French; the Drummonds probably spoke better than them. I knew no English or Italian at all apart from "do not lean outside" and "è pericoloso sporgersi," inscribed on train windows underneath "ne pas se pencher au-dehors." We thought it strange that a family who was well-off should choose to sleep out in the open rather than at a hotel. I imagined myself dead with my parents by the side of the road.

From that year, I still have two photographs. One shows me in my Communion dress. It's an "artistic portrait" in black and white, stuck on to a cardboard back with raised scrolls, covered by a semi-transparent sheet of paper. Inside—the signature of the photographer. You can see a girl with full, smooth features, high cheekbones, a rounded nose with large nostrils. A pair of glasses with heavy, light-colored frames bars her cheekbones. Her eyes are staring intently at the camera. The short permed hair sticks out from the back and the front of her Communion cap, loosely tied under her chin; from this cap hangs the veil. Just the hint of a smile at the corner of her mouth. The face of a conscientious little girl, looking older than her age because of the spectacles and permed hair. She is kneeling on a *prie-dieu* with her elbows on the padded cushion and her broad hands—a ring surrounds her little finger—locked under her chin, circled by a rosary falling down on to the missal and gloves lying on the armrest. There's something vague and nondescript about the figure in the muslin dress, whose belt has been tied loosely, just like the Communion cap. It seems there is no body underneath this small nun's habit because I cannot imagine it, let alone feel it the way I have come to feel mine. Yet, surprisingly, it's exactly the same body as the one I have today.

This photograph is dated June 5, 1952. It was taken not on the day of my solemn Communion in 1951 but, for some reason, on the day marking the "renewal of the vows," when the whole ceremony, including the costume, is repeated one year later.

In the other photograph, a small oblong one, I am pictured with my father in front of a low wall decorated with earthenware jars of flowers. It was taken in Biarritz in late August '52, no doubt somewhere along the promenade running by the sea hidden from view, during a bus trip to Lourdes. I can't be taller than one meter sixty: my head comes slightly higher than my father's shoulder and he was one meter seventy-three. In those three months my hair has grown, forming a sort of frizzy crown kept tight around my head by a ribbon. The photograph is blurred; it was taken with the cube-shaped camera my parents won at a fair before the war. Although one cannot clearly make out my face or my spectacles, a beaming smile is discernible. I am dressed in a white skirt and blouse—the uniform I wore for the Christian Youth Movement gathering. Over my shoulders—a jacket with its sleeves hanging. Here I appear to be slim, lean, because the skirt hugs my hips, then flares out. In this outfit, I look like a little woman. My father has on a dark jacket, pale shirt and pants, a somber tie. He is barely smiling, with that anxious look he has in all photographs. I imagine that I kept this snapshot because it was different from the others, portraying us as chic people, holiday-makers, which of course we weren't. In both photographs I am smiling with my lips closed because of my decayed, uneven teeth.

I stare at the two photographs until my mind goes blank, as if looking at them for long enough might allow me to slip into the head and body of the little girl who, one day, was there in the photographer's studio, or beside her father in Biarritz. Yet, if I had never seen these pictures before and if I were shown them for the first time, I would never believe that the little girl is me. (Absolute certainty—"yes, that's me"; total disbelief—"no, that's not me.")

The two pictures were taken barely three months apart. The first one at the beginning of June, the second one at the end of August. The format and quality are too different to reveal any significant change in my face or figure but I like to think of them as two milestones: one shows me in my Communion dress, closing off my childhood days; the other one introduces the era when I shall never cease to feel ashamed. It may be that I just need to single out part of that summer period, in the manner of a historian. (To write about "that summer" or "the summer of my twelfth year" is to romanticize events that could never feature in a novel, no more than the current summer '95; I cannot imagine any of these days ever belonging to the magical world conveyed by the expression "that summer.")

I have found further material evidence dating from that year:

a postcard with a black and white photograph of Elizabeth II. It was given to me by the daughter of a couple living in Le Havre, friends of my parents, who had been on a school trip to England to attend the coronation ceremony. On the back—a small brown stain, which was already there when she gave me the card and which I found quite repulsive. Every time I came across the card, I would think about the brown stain. Elizabeth II is pictured in profile, gazing into the distance, with short black hair combed backwards, her full lips outlined in ruby. Her left hand is resting on a fur coat; her right hand is holding a fan. I can't remember whether I thought she was beautiful. The question was immaterial since she was the Queen.

a small sewing kit in red leather, without its accessories— scissors, crochet hook, bodkin and so on—a Christmas present I had chosen instead of a desk blotter because it would be more useful at school.

a postcard showing the inside of Limoges Cathedral which I sent to my mother during the bus trip to Lourdes. On the back, in big letters: "In Limoges, the hotel is very nice, lots of foreigners come here. Love and kisses," with my name and "Papa." My father had written the address. The postmark reads 08/22/52.

a book of postcards—"The Castle in Lourdes—Museum of Pyrenean Arts and Customs"—which I probably bought when we visited the museum.

the sheet music for *Miami Beach Rhumba*, a blue double spread with little boats on the cover, bearing the names of artists who had sung or performed the song, namely Patrice and Mario, the Étienne sisters, Marcel Azzola and Jean Sablon. I guess I really loved that song as I longed to have the lyrics, contriving to persuade my mother to give me money for something which she saw as both trivial and useless for school, especially the latter. It certainly meant more to me than the summer hits *Ma p'tite folie* and *Mexico*, which one of the drivers would hum during our bus trip to Lourdes.

the vesperal pictured underneath my gloves in the Communion photograph—*Missel vespéral romain* by Dom Gaspard Lefebvre, Bruges. Each page is divided into two columns, Latin-French, except for the middle of the book, taken up by the "Ordinary of the Mass": here the right-hand page is in French, the left-hand page in Latin. The beginning features the "Roman Catholic Calendar of Secular Holidays and Movable Feasts from 1951 to 1968." Strange dates indeed; the book is so timeless it could have been written centuries ago. The same words keep reappearing and still mean nothing to me—secret, gradual, tract (I don't remember ever having tried to understand them). Sheer amazement, verging on unease as I leaf through this book written in what seems to me to be an esoteric language. I know all the words and I could reel off the *Agnus Dei* or any other short prayer by heart, yet I cannot identify with the little girl who, on Sundays and feast days, would recite Mass with seriousness or even fervor, assuming it would be a sin not to do so. Just like the two photographs are proof of my body in 1952, this missal—the fact that it has survived so many moves is in itself significant—provides indisputable evidence of the religious world to which I once belonged but which fails to move me today. *Miami Beach Rhumba* doesn't spark off the same feelings of unease because it's about love and traveling, two ambitions that are still part of my life. I

have just been humming the lyrics with great satisfaction—
*Ay, ay, ay, ay / It will thrill me / When I take a flight through
the sky / To Miami by the sea / Ay, ay, ay, ay / It will thrill me /
To fly to the place / Where my love waits for me.*

For the past few days, I have been living with that Sunday
in June. When I wrote about it, I could see it "in focus,"
with well-defined shapes and colors; I could even hear the
voices. Now it has become gray, incoherent and mute, like a
movie shown on crypted television without a decoder. The
fact that I have put it into writing does not make it any
more significant. It remains what it has always been since
1952—something akin to madness and death, to which I
have never ceased to compare the other events in my life in
order to assess their degree of painfulness, without finding
anything that could measure up to it.

If, as it now seems from a number of indications (needing
to reread the lines I have written, being unable to undertake
anything else), I have indeed started a new book, then I have
taken the risk of revealing it all straight away. Yet nothing is
revealed, only the stark facts. That day is like an icon
immured within me all these years; I would like to breathe

some life into it and strip it of its sacred aura (which long made me believe that it was responsible for my writing, that it lies somewhere at the heart of all my books).

I expect nothing from psychoanalysis or therapy, whose rudimentary conclusions became clear to me a long time ago—a domineering mother, a father whose submissiveness is shattered by a murderous gesture.... To state "it's a child-hood trauma" or "that day the idols were knocked off their pedestal" does nothing to explain a scene which could only be conveyed by the expression that came to me at the time: to *breathe disaster*. Here abstract speech fails to reach me.

Yesterday I went to the archives in Rouen to consult copies of the 1952 *Paris-Normandie* newspaper, which the delivery boy from the local news dealer brought round to my parents' house every day. This too was something which I could not face doing before, as if I would *breathe disaster* again simply by opening the June edition of the paper. As I climbed the stairs, I felt that I was heading toward some fearful encounter. In a room nestling under the eaves of the Town Hall a woman brought me two big black registers containing all the back issues published in 1952. I began reading from January 1. I wanted to delay the moment when I would reach June 15; I wanted to re-enter the innocent unfolding of days I had known before that date.

In the top right-hand corner of the first page was the weather forecast of Abbé Gabriel. There was nothing I could associate with it—no games, no walks, no bicycle rides. I did not feature in this drifting of clouds, sunny with bright intervals, strong winds, that punctuated the passing of time.

Although most of the events mentioned were known to me—the war in Indochina, the Korean conflict, the riots at Orléansville, Antoine Pinay's economic program—I wouldn't have set them in 1952, having no doubt memorized them at a later stage in my life. I could find no connection between "Six bicycles loaded with plastic explosive blow up in Saigon" or "Jacques Duclos imprisoned at Fresnes and indicted on charges of plotting against security of the state" and the images I had of myself in 1952. I found it strange to think that Stalin, Churchill and Eisenhower were once as real to me as Yeltsin, Clinton and Kohl are today. Nothing looked familiar. As if I hadn't lived in those days.

Gazing at the photograph of Antoine Pinay, I was struck by his resemblance to Valéry Giscard d'Estaing, not the decrepit man of today, but that of twenty years ago. The expression "Iron Curtain" took me back to the days of my Catholic school, when the mistress would tell us to recite a decade on our rosary for the Christians who were behind it: I would imagine a huge metal wall with men and women hurling themselves against it.

On the other hand, I immediately recognized the strip cartoon *Poustiquet*, similar to the ones published on the back page of *France-Soir* for so many years, and the joke of the day, wondering whether it used to make me laugh: "Well, then, young man, are the fish biting?—Oh no, Sir! These are yellowtail and they're as cute as can be!" I also recognized the advertisements and the names of movies showing in Rouen before they came to Y—*September Affair*, *Ma Femme est formidable* and so on.

There were horrific news items every day: a two-year-old had died eating a croissant; a farmer had sliced off the legs of his son, playing hide-and-seek in the wheat fields; a bombshell had killed three children in Creil. This was what I wanted to read about most of all.

The price of milk and butter made front-page news. Agricultural issues seemed to feature prominently, illustrated by information on foot-and-mouth disease, reports about farmers' wives and ads for veterinary products, Lapicrine, Osporcine. Judging by the number of throat lozenges and syrups that were advertised, people seemed to suffer from chronic coughing or else they relied exclusively on these products to get better instead of consulting a doctor.

The Saturday edition had a column called "Ladies' Choice." I seemed to detect a vague likeness between some of the jackets pictured here and the one I was wearing in the Biarritz snapshot. However, as regards the other clothes, I was sure that neither myself nor my mother had ever dressed that way and among the different hairstyles reproduced on that page I could not see the frazzled, crown-shaped perm I had in the photograph.

I got to the weekend edition dated Saturday 14-Sunday 15 June. The headlines read: "Wheat harvest up an estimated 10%—No favorites for the 24-hour race at Le Mans— Jacques Duclos undergoes lengthy questioning in Paris— Joëlle's body is found near her parents' house after a ten-day search. She had been thrown into an outdoor latrine by a neighbor who confessed to the crime."

I did not feel like reading on any further. Walking down-stairs, I realized that I had gone to the archives thinking I might actually find some record of what had happened to me in the 1952 newspaper. Later on, I reflected with astonishment that at the same time a continuous stream of cars had been roaring round the racetrack at Le Mans. I found it impossible to equate the two images. Then I said to myself that not one of the billion events that had happened somewhere in the world that Sunday afternoon could stand the comparison without producing the same feelings of dismay. Only the scene I had witnessed was real to me.

I have before me the list of events, films and advertisements that I jotted down with satisfaction while I was leafing through *Paris-Normandie.* I can expect nothing from this sort of document. Pointing out that cars and refrigerators were scarce and that 9 out of 10 screen stars used Lux Toilet Soap in 1952 is no more relevant than listing the different types of computer, microwave oven and frozen food that characterize the 1990s. The social distribution of goods is far more significant than their actual existence. In 1952, what mattered was that some did not have running water when others had bathrooms; today what matters is that some buy their clothes from Froggy when others go to Agnès B. When it comes to illustrating social change, newspapers can provide only collective evidence.

My overriding concern is to find the words I would use to describe myself and the world around me; to name what I considered to be normal, intolerable or inconceivable. But the woman of 1995 can never go back to being the little girl of 1952, who knew nothing beyond her small town, her family and her convent school, and who had a limited number of words at her disposal. With the immensity of time stretching ahead of her. We have no true memory of ourselves.

To convey what my life was like in those days, the only reliable method I have is to explore the laws, rites, beliefs and references that defined the circles in which I was caught up—school, family, small-town life—and which governed my existence, without my even noticing its contradictions; to expose the different languages that made up my personality: the words of religion, the words my parents used to describe their behavior and daily environment, the serialized novels I read in *Le Petit Écho de la mode* or *Les Veillées des chaumières*; to use these words, some of which I still find oppressive, in order to dissect and reassemble the text of the world surrounding that Sunday in June, when I turned twelve and thought I was going mad.

Naturally I shall not opt for narrative, which would mean inventing reality instead of searching for it. Neither shall I content myself with merely picking out and transcribing the images I remember; I shall process them like documents, examining them from different angles to give them meaning. In other words, I shall carry out an ethnological study of myself.

(It may not be necessary to commit such observations to paper, but I won't be able to start writing properly until I have some idea of the shape this writing will take.)

I may have chosen to be impartial because I thought the indescribable events I witnessed in my twelfth year would fade away, lost in the universal context of laws and language. Or maybe I succumbed to a mad and deadly impulse suggested by the words of a missal which I now find impossible to read, a ritual which my mind associates with some sort of Voodoo ceremony—*take this, all of you, and read it, this is my body, this is the cup of my blood, it will be shed for you and for all men.*

In June '52, I had never left the stretch of land commonly referred to as *these parts*, an expression understood by all despite its vagueness—the Pays de Caux, running along the right bank of the Seine, squeezed in between Le Havre and Rouen. Beyond that lay uncertainty, along with the rest of France and the world, dismissed as *over there* with a sweeping gesture toward the horizon, conveying indifference and the impossibility of ever living there. The only way to visit Paris is on a package tour, unless one has relatives to show one round the city. Taking the subway is seen as a complicated process, far more terrifying than the ghost train at the local fair, supposedly requiring a difficult and lengthy training. The general belief is that one cannot go anywhere that is not *familiar*, people feel genuine admiration for those who *aren't afraid of going places*.

The two big cities from around *these parts*, Le Havre and

Rouen, arouse less suspicion; they are inscribed in the linguistic memory of all families and belong to ordinary conversation. Many factory hands work there, leaving in the morning and coming back in the evening with the *micheline*, a small local train. In Rouen, the larger city, closer to us than Le Havre, *they've got everything you need*—department stores, specialists for every type of complaint, several movie theaters, an indoor pool for learning how to swim, the Saint-Romain festival lasting the month of November, tramways, tea rooms and huge hospitals where people are taken for major operations, detoxification programs and electroshock treatment. Unless you happen to be a laborer working on a building site, you would never go there in your "everyday" clothes. My mother takes me there once a year to consult the eye specialist and buy me a pair of glasses. She takes advantage of the trip to purchase beauty care products and other articles "you can't get in Y." We never feel quite at home there because we don't know anyone. People appear to dress and speak better than in the country. In Rouen, one always feels slightly "at a disadvantage"—less sophisticated, less intelligent and, generally speaking, less gracious with one's body and speech. For me, Rouen symbolizes the future, just like serialized novels and fashion magazines do.

In 1952 my whole life centers around Y—its streets, its stores and its inhabitants, for whom I am Annie D or "the D's girl." For me there *is* no other world. Y is the underlying reference in all conversations; its schools, church, fairs and ladies' fashion stores dictate our social status and our ambitions. With its seven thousand inhabitants, this town lying half-way between Le Havre and Rouen is the only one where we can say, referring to a great many people, "he or she lives on that street, works there, has so many children," where we can reel off the times for Mass and the movies showing at the Cinéma Leroy, where we know who is the best baker or the least dishonest butcher. Because my parents were born there and, before that, their own parents and grandparents in villages nearby, there is no other town which we knew so intimately both historically and geographically. I know who lived next door fifty years ago and where my mother would buy bread on the way back from school. In the street I pass men and women whom my mother and father almost married before they met. People "who aren't from around these parts" are those we have no knowledge of at all, whose story is either unknown or cannot be checked, and who in turn know nothing about us. Be they from Brittany, Marseilles or Spain, anyone who doesn't speak "the way we do" is, to some extent, labeled a foreigner.

(I find it impossible to name this town, as I have done

in previous books. Here it is not a geographical landmark on a map, lying somewhere between Rouen and Le Havre, cut across by the railroad tracks or highway N15. It is a nameless place of origin: as soon as I go back I succumb to a state of lethargy that prevents me from thinking or even remembering, as if the place were going to swallow me up once again.)

Description of Y in 1952.

The town center, razed by a fire during the German advance in 1940 and subsequently bombed in 1944 like the rest of Normandy, is undergoing reconstruction. It features a combination of construction sites, wasteland, recent concrete buildings—two stories high with new businesses at street level—temporary shacks and early edifices spared by the war: the Town Hall, the Cinéma Leroy, the post office and the covered market. The church was burned down: a small playhouse on the main square is used in its stead. Mass is celebrated on stage, before people seated in the orchestra or in the gallery running around the room.

The town center is circled by a network of cobbled and tarred streets, lined with sidewalks, two-story houses in brick or stone and mansions behind closed gates, belonging to lawyers, doctors and company directors. This is where the public and private schools are to be found, located in their respective neighborhoods. Although this area lies outside the center, it is still part of town. Beyond live the people who say they are going "to town" or even "to Y" when they pay a visit to the center. There are no clear geographical boundaries separating the city center from the other districts: the disappearance of sidewalks, more and more vegetable gardens and old houses (with half-timbering, two or three rooms, no more, no running water, an outdoor toilet), hardly any stores at all except a café-grocery-coal depot, the first housing developments. The practical implications of this distinction, however, are clear to all: the city center is where you don't go shopping in your slippers or your overalls. The neighborhoods lose in value the further one strays from the city center—fewer and fewer villas, more and more blocks of houses clustered around a shared courtyard. The more remote areas, with dirt tracks, potholes in rainy weather and farmhouses fronted by embankments, already belong to the country.

The Clos-des-Parts neighborhood extends lengthwise from the town center to Cany bridge, running from the rue de la République to the Champ-des-Courses district. Its main axis is the rue du Clos-des-Parts, which connects the route du Havre to Cany bridge, cutting across the heart of the city.

My parents' store is located at the lower end of the street—we would "go up to town"—on the corner of a graveled alley opening on to the rue de la République. So one can take either the latter or the rue du Clos-des-Parts to go to the private school: the two streets are parallel. They have absolutely nothing in common. The rue de la République, wide, tarred, flanked by sidewalks from end to end, is used by cars or buses heading for the coast and the beaches twenty-five kilometers away. The upper stretch of the road features stately residences; no one knows the people who live there, not even "by sight." The presence of a Citroën garage, a few adjoining houses giving straight on to the street and a bicycle repair store at the lower end do not detract from its noble character. On the right, before reaching the bridge, below the railroad line, lie two huge ponds with a narrow dirt track running in between; one is filled with black water, the other one has a greenish tinge because of the moss sprouting on its surface. It's known as the "traveler's pond," the death spot of Y; women come over from the other end of town to drown here. As you can't see it from the rue de la République, from which it is separated by an embankment crowned by a thick hedge, it doesn't appear to be part of the street.

The rue du Clos-des-Parts is a narrow, uneven street, with no sidewalks, characterized by sudden dips and sharp bends; it has practically no traffic except for workers cycling home in the evening, cutting across to join the route du Havre. In the afternoon, it offers the silence and faraway sounds of the country. There are a few villas belonging to entrepreneurs, with adjoining workshops, and many single-story buildings standing side by side, rented out to clerks or manual workers. Four winding paths inaccessible to cars branch off the rue du Clos-des-Parts, serving the huge Champ-de-Courses neighborhood that extends to the race-course, dominated by the sheer mass of the old people's home. It's a shaded district with hedges and gardens fronting old houses: there are more elderly people, "lower-income groups" and large families here than anywhere else. From the rue de la République to the paths cutting across Champ-de-Courses, it takes less than three hundred meters to switch from wealth to poverty, from city life to country life, from space to confinement. To switch from protected people, of whom we know nothing, to people of whom we know everything—the welfare benefits they receive, what they eat and drink, what time they go to bed.

(To describe for the very first time, with no criterion other than accuracy, streets along which I used to walk as a child without ever thinking about them, is to expose the social hierarchy they implied. I almost feel I am committing a sacrilege: replacing the sweet landscape of memory—a whirl of impressions, colors and images (the Edelin Villa! the blue wisteria! the blackberry bushes in Champ-de-Courses!)—by a far harsher one that strips it of all magic, but whose truth cannot be questioned, not even by memory: in 1952 I could tell simply by looking at the lofty façades tucked away behind lawns and gravel paths that the people living there *were not like us*.)

Our place still refers to:
1) the neighborhood
2) the house and store belonging to my parents, in my mind inextricably linked.

The grocery-haberdashery-café is in a group of old, low houses with yellow and brown half-timbering, flanked at each end by a recent two-story building in brick, on a strip of land stretching from the rue de la République to the rue du Clos-des-Parts. We live in the part that opens on to the latter street, together with an elderly gardener who is allowed to walk through our courtyard. The grocery store, with its single bedroom upstairs, is housed in the new building made of brick. The front entrance and one of the store windows give on to the rue du Clos-des-Parts; another window faces the courtyard, which one walks through to enter the café, set up in the original farmhouse. The store opens on to a series of four rooms: the kitchen, the café, the cellar and a junk room known as the "back room"; all these rooms communicate with each other and the courtyard (except the kitchen, squeezed in between the grocery and the café). None of the first-floor rooms afford any privacy whatsoever, not even the kitchen, which customers use as a shortcut to get to the café. The fact that there is no door between the café and the kitchen means that my parents can keep on talking to customers, who also have the benefit of our radio. From the kitchen, a winding staircase leads to a tiny loft with the bedroom on the left and the attic on the right. In this room belongs the bucket used as a chamber pot by my mother and myself, and by my father at night (in the daytime he and the customers use a urinal set up in the courtyard—a barrel surrounded by planks). The outdoor toilet is used by us in summer and by customers throughout the year. Except when it's a nice day and I can sit outside, I usually read and do my homework at the top of the stairs, under a light bulb. From there, I can see everything that goes on through the bars of the banister, without being seen.

The courtyard is a sort of wide passageway in beaten earth running between the house and the outbuildings used as storehouses. Behind these are a shed with rabbit hutches, a wash house, the toilet, a hen run and a small grassy patch.

(This is where I am sitting, one evening in late May or early June, before that Sunday. I have finished my homework; there is a pervading sweetness in the air. I feel intoxicated by the future. It's the same feeling I get when I sing *Mexico* and *Miami Beach Rhumba* in my bedroom at the top of my voice, the same feeling as when I marvel at the mystery of a whole lifetime stretching ahead of me.)

Walking back from town, as soon as we catch sight of the grocery store, jutting out on to the street, my mother says: *We are approaching the palace.* (Out of pride as much as derision.)

The store is open all year from seven o' clock in the morning to nine o' clock at night, continuously except on Sunday afternoons, when it stays closed; the café re-opens at six. The comings and goings of customers, along with their lifestyle and their occupation, command our working hours, both in the café (men) and in the store (women). A short lull in the afternoon, breaking up the constant bustle of the day. My mother uses the spare time to make her bed, recite a prayer or sew on a button; my father goes off to tend the large vegetable garden he rents nearby.

Practically all my parents' customers come from the lower end of the rue de la République and the rue du Clos-des-Parts, the Champ-des-Courses neighborhood and a semi-industrial, semi-rural area extending beyond the railroad line. This includes a district known as the Corderie, named after a rope factory where my parents used to work when they were young, converted after the war into a workshop for the clothing industry and a plant manufacturing bird cages. It's a single street, running below the railroad tracks; after going past the factories, it opens out on to a clearing where hundreds of wooden planks are piled up high, waiting to be made into cages. This is family territory: my mother lived here as a teenager until she got married; one of her brothers, two of her sisters and her mother still live here. The house occupied by my grandmother, one of my aunts and her husband, once served as the factory canteen, as well as a locker room: a raised hut on stilts with five tiny rooms and no electricity, where the floor vibrates and resonates loudly. On New Year's Day the whole family congregates in my grandmother's room, the grown-ups gathered around the table, drinking and singing, the children bouncing on the bed against the wall. On Sundays when I was a very little girl, my mother would take me to see my grandmother, then we would go to uncle Joseph's house, where I would play seesaw with my cousins, balancing on the huge planks, or sit down and wave at the trains going to Le Havre, or tease any boys we met by *calling them names*. I seem to remember that we weren't going there so often in 1952.

Moving down from the town center to the rue du Clos-des-Parts or, further still, to the Corderie neighborhood means switching from a world where people know how to speak properly to a world where they don't, expressing themselves in a mix of standard French and local dialect, according to the speaker's age, occupation and ambition to better him or herself. The dialect, virtually the only means of expression for elderly people like my grandmother, would be conveyed by the odd phrase or intonation in the case of office girls. Everybody, including those who speak it, agree that the dialect is both ugly and old-fashioned but they give the following excuse: "we know the right expression but it's so much quicker this way." Speaking properly implies making an effort, searching for a new word instead of using the first one that springs to mind and taking on a softer, more cautious voice, as if one were handling a precious object. Most adults don't think it necessary to "speak good French"; it's something they associate with the younger generation. My father often says, "ain't seen him" or "ain't heard him"; when I correct him, he repeats "I-did-not-see-him" slowly, deliberately spacing out the syllables, adding in his usual voice, "if you say so"—a concession that shows how little he cares about speaking properly.

In 1952 although I write "correct" French, I probably say "all what I know" and "to scrub" instead of "to wash," just like my parents, since we share the same experience of the world. It is defined by familiar gestures—the way we sit down, laugh and grab hold of objects—and familiar words telling us what to do with our body and the things around us. We all knew how:

—not to *throw away food* but to make the most of it: cutting up bread into small squares next to one's plate to soak up the gravy; if the mashed potatoes are too hot, starting by the edge of the plate or blowing on the food to make it cool; tilting the plate so that one's spoon catches all the broth or grabbing it with both hands and sucking up the soup; taking sips to cram down the food

—to stay clean without *wasting the water*: using a single basin to wash one's face, teeth and hands, and in summer one's legs because they got grubby; wearing clothes that *keep the dirt*

—to slaughter and prepare animals for human consumption with sharp, accurate movements: thumping rabbits behind the ear with one's fist; squeezing a chicken between one's legs and plunging an open pair of scissors down its throat; holding a duck down on to the block and chopping its head off with a scythe

—to express silent contempt: shrugging one's shoulders, turning round and vigorously slapping one's ass.

Instances of daily behavior that distinguish men from women:

—placing the iron close to one's cheek to see how hot it is; kneeling down on all fours to scrub the floor or standing with one's legs wide apart to pick weeds for the rabbits; sniffing one's panties and stockings at the end of the day

—spitting into one's hands before grabbing hold of the spade; shoving a cigarette behind one's ear for later on; sitting astride chairs; snapping one's penknife shut before slipping it into one's pocket.

Polite phrases such as, *It's a pleasure! Have a nice day!* or *Have a seat, we won't charge extra.*

Sentences magically linking our body to the universe or to our destiny—*there's an eyelash on your cheek, you'd better make a wish; my left ear is popping, someone's saying nice things about me*—as well as to nature—*my corn is hurting, it's going to rain.*

Affectionate or stern threats said to children: *I'll box your ears; get down from there or I'll smack your face.*

Mocking remarks to ward off demonstrations of affection: *get lost; give me a break; run along, I don't need your fleas!*

Because of the dusty color associated with post-war demolition and reconstruction, black and white movies and textbooks, and dark fur-lined jackets and overcoats, I see the year 1952 as being uniformly gray, like former East

European countries. Yet there were roses, clematis and wisteria growing over fences in our neighborhood, and blue dresses with red patterns like the one my mother wore. The wallpaper in the café had pink flowers. The sun was shining on that Sunday. It's just that it is a silent, ritual world where isolated sounds, linked to people's daily routine, punctuate time and the passing of seasons: the Angelus bell of the old people's home summoning its residents to get up or go to bed; the siren of the textile factory; the cars on market day; the barking of dogs and the dull thud of the spade hitting the earth in spring.

Each week is divided into "days for ..." defined by social and family habit, as well as by radio programs. Monday—dead day, stale bread and leftovers, *Le Crochet radiophonique* on Radio Luxembourg. Tuesday—washing day, *Reine d'un jour.* Wednesday—market day, the poster announcing the next movie at the Cinéma Leroy, *Quitte ou double.* Thursday—my day off, a new copy of *Lisette.* Friday—fish day. Saturday—scrubbing the house, washing our hair. Sunday—Mass, the supreme ritual governing all others, a change of underwear, a new outfit, cakes from the baker plus our "special treat," minor pains and pleasures.

Every evening of the week, at twenty minutes past seven, we listened to *La Famille Duraton* on the radio.

A lifetime is split up into successive stages when people become "old enough to":

—take Holy Communion and receive their first watch, have their hair permed in the case of girls, wear their first suit in the case of boys

—start having their period and be allowed to wear stockings

—drink wine at family gatherings, be allowed a cigarette, listen when grown-ups tell rude stories

—get a job and go dancing, start "seeing" boys or girls

—do one's military service

—go and see naughty films

—get married and have kids

—wear black

—stop working

—die.

In our lives nothing is thought, everything is done.

People are forever remembering. Their conversation inevitably begins with "before the war" or "during the war." No family or social gathering takes place without the Rout, the Occupation or the bombings being mentioned. Each person plays their part in retracing the great epic, describing their personal feelings of panic or horror, reminiscing about the bitter winter of 1942, the rutabaga and the air raid warnings, mimicking the drone of V2 missiles patrolling the sky. The Exodus gives rise to the more lyrical accounts, invariably ending with "when the next war comes around, I'm staying home" or "we never want to see that again." In the café arguments break out between the men who were gassed during World War I and those taken prisoner in 1939-1944, dismissed as cowards by the former.

Yet they never stop talking about *progress*, seen as an inexorable driving force which cannot and must not be opposed, evidenced by more and more new products: plastic, nylon stockings, the ball-point pen, Vespa motorcycles, dried soup and free education for all.

At the age of twelve I was living by the rules and codes of this world; it never occurred to me that there might be others.

Because children were thought to be naturally malicious, chastising them and teaching them how to behave was the duty of all good parents. Be it a "box on the ear" or a "proper spanking," corporal punishment was encouraged. This didn't imply that parents were harsh or spiteful, so long as they didn't overdo it and took pains to spoil the child in other ways. When parents were telling about how they had disciplined their child for doing something wrong, they would often end the story with a proud "I almost did him in!" satisfied at having given him a good hiding and having contained the fatal outburst of anger which such malevolence would nonetheless have warranted. Fearing no doubt that he might "do me in," my father refused to lay a finger on me, or even reprimand me, leaving this role to my mother. *You slob! You little brat! Life will sort you out all right!*

People were continually spying on each other. It was essential to learn about other people's lives, so that they could be talked about, and to protect one's own, so that it couldn't be. It was a tricky balance, "worming information out of someone" but not letting them do the same in return, or else just "saying what you could afford to reveal." Socializing was people's favorite distraction. They loved to mingle with the crowds pouring out of movie theaters or rushing off the station platform at night. The mere fact that people congregated somewhere was a good enough reason for joining in. A brass band or a bicycle race provided an opportunity to enjoy not only the event but also the sight of the crowd, and to go home saying who had been there and with whom. People's conduct was scrutinized and their behavior analyzed in minute detail, including the most personal traits; these signs were gathered and interpreted, shaping the history of other people. A sort of collective novel, with each of us making our contribution, adding the odd detail or a few narrative flourishes to the general picture, which people in the store or around the table usually summed up by "he's a good guy" or "she ain't worth much."

Conversation classified people's actions and behavior, slotting them into categories—good or bad, permissible, sometimes even encouraged, and inadmissible. There was an outright condemnation of divorcees, Communists, unmarried couples, single mothers, women who drank, who got an abortion, whose heads were shaved at the Liberation, who didn't keep their house tidy and so on. Lesser disapproval was shown toward girls who got pregnant before they married, men who *had a good time at the café* (to *have a good time* was the privilege of children and young people) and masculine demeanor generally. People showing courage at work were praised; although it didn't remedy their bad ways, it made them more acceptable: *he drinks but he's hard working*. Health was seen as a virtue; *she has poor health* was as much a reproach as a sign of sympathy. Illness was invariably tinged with guilt, as if people had somehow been neglectful with their lives. There was a strong reluctance to accept that people could be justifiably and genuinely sick; instead they would be accused of *fussing over themselves*.

Storytelling involved an element of horror that came across as natural, or even necessary, as if to warn people of some terrible fatality—accident or disease—which they had little chance of escaping. The narrative resorted to powerful images which would remain imprinted in one's memory: "she sat down on two vipers" or "one of his skull bones is growing soft." More often than not, these nasty twists were unexpected, in lieu of a happier, more predictable ending: children are quietly playing with a shiny object that turns out to be a bombshell and so on.

Being easily shocked, being *excitable*, served only to arouse suspicion and curiosity. The best thing was to say, *it didn't do a thing to me.*

People were judged by their ability to socialize. One had to be simple, straightforward and polite. Children who behaved in an "underhanded way" and workers with a "quarrelsome temper" failed to observe the rules of normal conversation. Those who kept to themselves were looked down on and accused of boorishness. Wanting to live alone (contempt for bachelors and spinsters) and refusing to speak to others was seen as the denial of an act that carried human dignity: *they live like savages!* Besides, it clearly showed that one took no interest in what was undoubtedly the most interesting of all things—other people's lives. And therefore that one *ignored social convention.* On the other hand, spending too much time with neighbors or friends, "always hanging out with so-and-so" was just as bad: it showed one had no pride.

Politeness was the supreme virtue, the basic principle underlying all social behavior. It involved, for instance:
—reciprocating an invitation or a gift; observing the order of precedence for age when wishing the family a Happy New Year; taking care not to *disturb* people by dropping round unexpectedly or by asking them personal questions; taking care not to *insult* them by refusing an invitation or a biscuit. Being polite meant that one was *on good terms* with everyone and that one never gave rise to gossip: looking straight ahead when one crossed the courtyard didn't mean that one wasn't curious but that one didn't want to be caught peering into other people's houses. Salutations exchanged in the street, greetings one was either granted or denied and the manner in which these rituals were performed (speaking in jocular or curt tones, stopping to shake hands, saying a few words or else walking straight on) were scrupulously analyzed, prompting all manner of assumptions—*he can't have seen me, he must have been in a hurry.* Those who ignored the existence of their peers by *refusing to look at people* were beyond forgiveness.

A façade against the outside world, social graces were unnecessary between husband and wife, parents and children; at home they were seen as a manifestation of hypocrisy or even malevolence. Harshness, aggressiveness and grousing were the usual means of communication among families.

To be like everyone else was people's universal ambition, the ultimate dream. Those who were different were thought to be eccentric or even *deranged.* The dogs in our neighborhood were all called Rover or Spot.

In the café-grocery store we live surrounded by "people"— our way of referring to the customers. They can see us taking our meals and leaving for church or for school; they can hear us washing in a corner of the kitchen and peeing in the bucket. Because we are continually exposed to them, we need to be on our best behavior (no insults, no rude words, no gossip) and to contain our emotion, anger or grief, concealing anything that might excite envy or curiosity, anything likely to be *talked about.* We know quite a few things about our customers, for instance, how much they earn and what sort of life they lead; it is agreed, however, that they must know nothing about us, or only the bare minimum. So, "in front of people," it is forbidden to say how much we paid for a pair of shoes, to complain of stomach ache or to reel off my good grades at school: we always throw a dish towel over the baker's cake and slip the bottle of wine under the table as soon as anyone comes in. We wait until the last client has left before starting an argument. Otherwise, *what would people think?*

The code of behavior of the perfect storekeeper involves a number of rules; the following ones apply to me:
—I must say hello in a clear, loud voice every time I enter or walk through the store or the café
—I must be first to greet customers wherever I meet them
—I must not repeat the things I know about them, I must not speak ill of them or other storekeepers
—I must never divulge the takings of the day
—I must never *give myself airs* or *show off*

The penalty for the non-observance of these rules, however slight, was well known to me—*we'll lose customers because of you*, with the inevitable consequence, *we'll go bankrupt.*

Revealing the moral precepts of the world I knew as a twelve-year-old conjures up, albeit briefly, the indescribable oppressiveness and sense of confinement which I experience in my dreams. The words that come to me are opaque, stones too heavy to move. Empty of imagery. Empty of formal meaning such as a dictionary might provide. There is no fantasy, no perspective surrounding these words: they are only matter. Familiar words inextricably linked to people and things from my childhood, brittle words that leave me no leeway. Tables of the Law.

(The words that made me dream in 1952—*The Queen of Golconde, Sunset Boulevard, ice cream, pampa*—will never carry any weight; they still have that exotic, airy quality they had in my childhood, when they were shrouded in mystery. And all those adjectives one found in women's romances—a *haughty* bearing, to speak in *sullen, contemptuous, supercilious, sarcastic* or *bitter* tones—which in my mind could never apply to a real person or to anyone I knew. I believe that my writing is still confined to that material language of the past; the words and syntax which did not come to me at the time have never come to me. I shall never experience the pleasure of juggling with metaphors or indulging in stylistic play.)

There were hardly any words for describing emotion—*I was put straight* (disenchantment), I was *black as thunder* (discontent). *It grieved me* could mean being sorry to leave food on one's plate or being sad at losing one's sweetheart. And of course to *breathe disaster*. The language of feeling was to be found in the songs of Luis Mariano and Tino Rossi, in novels by Delly and in the serials published by *Le Petit Écho de la mode* and *La Vie en fleurs*.

I shall now describe the atmosphere of the private boarding-school where I spent most of my time and which played a decisive role in my life, bringing together and equating two necessities, two ideals—knowledge and religion.

I was the only one in the family to have a private education; my cousins in Y went to a public school, so did all the girls from my neighborhood, except maybe for two or three of the older ones.

A large building in dark red brick, the convent school took up the whole side of a quiet, somber street in the center of Y. Opposite lay the blank façades of warehouses that probably belonged to the post office. No windows at street level, only a few circular openings high up to let in the daylight and two doors, always closed. One was the porch through which pupils entered and left, giving on to a closed-in, heated playground that provided access to the chapel. The other door, at the far end of the building, was forbidden territory for pupils; you had to ring before being admitted by a Sister, who would take you to a small lobby facing the principal's office and the parlor. On the second story—a row of windows opening on to the classrooms and a corridor. The windows on the third floor and the skylights above were cloaked in white curtains. That's where the dormitories were located. It was forbidden to look out of any of the windows down into the street.

Unlike the state-run establishments located outside the town center, where children could be seen playing in huge courtyards behind closed gates, nothing that went on in the private school was visible from outside. There were two playgrounds. One, a cobbled area with no sun, made even darker by the foliage of a tall tree, was used by the few pupils enrolled in the "free school" curriculum: children coming from the orphanage next to the Town Hall and girls whose parents could not afford the school fees. There was only one schoolmistress in charge of this section, which went from second grade to sixth grade; very few girls actually made it to sixth grade as the large majority would go straight into "domestic science." The other playground, a large, sunny area reserved for the girls privately enrolled at the Catholic boarding-school (daughters of storekeepers, artisans and farmers) ran the whole length of the refectory and the covered play area that one crossed to reach the classrooms on the second floor. At one end it was sealed off by the chapel and its windows covered with wire mesh and, at the other, by a wall separating it from the free school, flanked by filthy toilets on either side. At the back of the courtyard, parallel to the main building, was a row of bushy lime trees; underneath these the little ones would play hopscotch and the older girls would study for their exams. Beyond the path lay a garden planted with fruit trees and vegetables, ending in a high wall which one could never see except in winter. The two playgrounds communicated through a crude opening in the wall that supported the toilets. The twenty or so pupils from the free school and the one hundred and fifty to two hundred from the private school never met except on special occasions and for solemn Communion; otherwise they had no contact whatsoever. The girls attending private school would immediately identify the other ones because of their clothes; sometimes they recognized items that had belonged to them, worn-out, relinquished garments that their parents had handed down to these needy girls.

The only men ordinarily allowed inside the Catholic school were the priests and the gardener, who was confined to the cellars and the grounds. Repairs requiring the presence of workers were carried out during the summer vacation. The principal and more than half the teaching staff were nuns; they wore dark non-religious clothes, black, brown or navy blue, and were addressed as "Mademoiselle." The other teachers, unmarried women with a touch of class in some cases, came from bourgeois families, notables or storekeepers living in the town center.

The following rules demand unquestioning obedience:
—we must line up in front of the playground when we hear the first bell, which our schoolmistresses take turns to ring, and troupe upstairs in silence when we hear the second bell five minutes later
—we must make sure we never touch the handrail
—we must rise to our feet whenever a teacher, a priest or the principal enters the classroom and remain in this position until they leave, except when they motion us to sit down; we must rush to open the door when they come in and close it behind them
—we must look down and incline our head and shoulders every time we address our schoolmistresses or walk past them, in the same way we bow before the holy sacrament in church
—none of the day girls and, during the day, none of the boarders is allowed upstairs into the dormitory. It is the

most secret place in the whole building. During all the years I spent at school, I never set foot there once —except for those who have a written dispensation from the doctor, it is forbidden to go and relieve oneself during class. (On the first day of term following the Easter break in 1952, I felt like going just after class had resumed in the afternoon. I somehow managed to hold back until recess, sweating heavily, on the verge of fainting, terrified of shitting in my pants.)

Instruction and religion are inseparably linked, both in time and in space. Except for the playground and the toilets, all areas of the school premises are conducive to prayer. The chapel, naturally enough, the classroom, with its crucifix hanging on the wall above the teacher's desk, the refectory and the garden, where, every year in May, the rosary is recited before a statue of the Virgin set up on a raised pedestal, nestling before a leafy trellis made to resemble the grotto in Lourdes. Prayers open and close all school activities. We recite them standing behind our desks, heads bent, fingers crossed, making the sign of the cross* at the beginning and end of each prayer. The longer prayers introduce morning

---

* This is done by using our right hand to touch our forehead, our chest, our left shoulder and our right shoulder, preferably with the rosary cross, which we raise to our lips at the end of the ritual.

and afternoon class. At half-past eight in the morning—*The Lord's Prayer, Hail Mary, I believe in God, Confiteor, Acts of Faith, Hope, Charity and Contrition,* and occasionally *Remember O most gracious Mary.* At half-past one in the afternoon—*The Lord's Prayer* and ten times *Hail Mary.* Shorter prayers, frequently replaced by canticles after recess, announce the end of morning and afternoon class. Boarders are allowed twice as many prayers, from the time they get up to the time they go to bed.

Prayer is the supreme act of life—the remedy for both individual and universal ills. We must pray to better ourselves, to overcome temptation, to get good grades in arithmetic, to heal the sick and to convert those who have sinned. Every morning since nursery school we have pursued our commentary of the same book—the Roman Catholic catechism. Religious instruction is the first subject listed on our report card. In the morning, the day is offered as a gift to God and all our activities are directed toward Him. Our aim in life is to achieve a permanent "state of grace."

On Saturday mornings one of the older girls goes round all the schoolrooms to collect our confession notes (a piece of paper on which we have written our name and classroom). The afternoon unfolds according to a set routine: the girl who has been granted absolution by the chaplain in the sacristy is given a note with the name of the pupil whom the chaplain wishes to receive and hear in confession. She goes straight to the classroom mentioned on the piece of paper and reads the name out loud; the girl stands up and goes to chapel and so on. The observance of religious practices (confession, Holy Communion) appears to take precedence over the acquisition of knowledge: "One can have top grades in all subjects and still displease God." At the end of term the archpriest, accompanied by the principal, reads out the school results and the honor roll; he gives the good pupils a big picture of a saint; the others get a small one. He signs the picture and inscribes the date on the back.

The chronology of our school activities is dictated by the chronology of the missal and the gospel, fixing the subject of the day's religious instruction class, before French dictation: the period around Advent and Christmas (a crib with figurines is set up by the window until Candlemas); the period around Lent, divided into Sundays (Septuagesima, Sexagesima); the period around Easter, Ascension and Pentecost. Day after day, year after year, the private school tells us the same story over and over again, cultivating familiarity with invisible yet omnipresent characters who are neither dead nor alive—the Virgin Mary, the Infant Jesus, the angels—whose lives are closer to us than those of our own grandparents.

(I feel compelled to use the present tense to list and describe these rules, as if they have remained as immutable as they were for me at the time. The more I explore this world of the past, the more dismayed I am by its coherence and its strength. Yet I am sure I was perfectly happy there and could aspire to nothing better. For its laws were lost in the sweet, pervasive smells of food and wax polish floating upstairs, the distant shouts coming from the playground and the morning silence shattered by the tinkling of a piano—a girl practicing scales with her music teacher.

Also, I must admit the following: up to my adolescence, nothing in the world could have changed the fact that for me faith in God was the norm and Roman Catholic religion the only truth. Although today I can read *Being and Nothingness* and be amused by *Charlie Hebdo*'s portrayal of Jean-Paul II as "the Polish transvestite," I can never forget that in 1952 I believed I had been living in a state of mortal sin since my First Communion because the host flaked on the roof of my mouth before I had time to swallow it. I was certain of having destroyed and desecrated what I thought was the body of God. Religion was my whole life. Believing and having to believe were the same thing.)

We live in a world of truth, a world of light and perfection. In the other world, people don't go to church or say their prayers: it's the world of those who have sinned. Its name, mentioned only on very rare occasions, rings out like a blasphemy: secular education. (For me the word "secular" had no definite meaning, it was vaguely synonymous with "bad.") We do everything to distinguish our world from the other one. We are supposed to say "refectory" instead of "canteen" and "sacristy" instead of "cloakroom." "Comrades" and "Miss" smack of secular education; we must say "our classmates" and "Mademoiselle," and address the principal as "dear Sister." None of the teachers say *tu* to their pupils and even the five-year-olds at kindergarten are addressed formally as *vous*.

Unlike public education, private education is characterized by a wealth of celebrations. Throughout the year, a large part of school time is taken up with the preparation for various events: at Christmas, a stage presentation in the indoor playground for pupils, with repeats for parents on the two following Sundays; in April, an alumni reunion including a trip to the local movie theater, with several evening performances for parents later on in the week; in June, a fete organized in Rouen by the Christian Youth Movement.

The most popular celebration is the parish fair in early July, heralded by a procession through the city streets, with all the girls dressed up in costumes around a chosen theme. With its flower-decked figures, circus riders and old-fashioned dames, singing and leaping, private education unveils its charms to the crowds lining the sidewalks, displaying imagination and unquestionable supremacy over public education—the latter had held its celebrations the week before, with pupils marching to the Champ-des-Courses neighborhood in their gym outfits. The parish fair seals the victory of private education.

During preparations for the fair, everything that is normally forbidden is permissible: going into town to buy material or to slip invitations into people's mailboxes; leaving the classroom before the end of the lesson to go and rehearse one's part. Although we are not allowed to come to school in trousers without wearing a skirt on top, on stage the little girls in tutus expose their naked thighs and panties, the older ones, the top of their breasts and the hair under their arms. The male gender is suggested by the disturbing figures of girls dressed up as men who kiss hands and declare their love.

At the Christmas show in 1951, I am one of the "La Rochelle girls" named after a traditional French song. Standing next to two or three other students, I sing facing the audience, motionless, holding a ship in my arms. Originally, I was to be one of the "three little drummer boys returning from war" but the Sister in charge of rehearsals sent me back because I couldn't march in time with the music. In April 1952, at the alumni reunion, I am featured in a Greek painting—a maiden making an offering to a dead girl. My body is bent forward, resting on one outstretched leg, the palms of my hands facing upward. I remember it as sheer torture; I dreaded that I would collapse on stage. Both roles were static and both involved minor characters, probably because I lacked grace, a fact evidenced by many photographs.

Everything that cements this world is encouraged, everything that threatens it is denounced and vilified. It is good form:

—to attend chapel during recess

—to make Communion privately at the age of seven instead of waiting for solemn Communion, like the girls who attend school without God

—to join the "Croisées," an organization whose mission is to convert people throughout the world, seen as the ultimate expression of religious fervor

—to carry around a rosary in one's pocket

—to buy a copy of *Âmes vaillantes*

—to own a copy of Dom Lefebvre's evening prayer book

—to say that "the whole family joins in the evening prayers" and that one wants to take the veil.

It is bad form:

—to come to school with books and magazines other than religious works such as *Âmes vaillantes*. Because of the existence of "bad books," reading in itself breeds suspicion; we are warned about these books and made to fear them, and they are even mentioned in the examination of conscience before confession. Consequently, we imagine them to be awesome and far more numerous than the good ones. The books handed out on prize-giving day, provided by the town's Catholic bookstore, are intended to be shown, not read. They edify those who merely glance at them. *The Bible for Children*, *Général de Lattre de Tassigny* and *Hélène Boucher* are the titles I remember.

—to mix with girls who attend public school

—to see movies other than those scheduled by the school (*Joan of Arc, Monsieur Vincent, The Bishop of Ars*). On the church door hangs the Index published by the Roman Catholic Church, classifying films in terms of dangerousness. Any girl seen coming out of a movie that had been "banned" was likely to be expelled then and there.

It is unthinkable to read photo romances or to go to the public dance held in the Poteaux hall on Sunday afternoons.

Yet these rules are never perceived as being coercive. Authority is exerted in a gentle, *convivial* manner, as through the encouraging smile of the "Mademoiselle" whom we meet in the street and greet with deference.

The pupils' parents exercise extreme vigilance in the streets of the town center in order to preserve the reputation of the private school and its key role in the selection process—details of what the girls wear and whom they meet will ultimately be *talked about*. Saying "my daughter goes to a private school" instead of simply "my daughter goes to school" emphasizes the difference between those who are thrown together indiscriminately and those who belong to a special world, between those merely attending compulsory education and those who early on have opted for a better life.

Naturally, it was understood that within the boundaries of the private school there were neither rich girls nor poor girls but one big Catholic family.

(For me the word *private* will always suggest deprivation, fear and lack of openness. Including in the expression *private life*. Writing is something public.)

In this world of excellence, I am acknowledged as an excellent student and I enjoy the freedom and privileges conferred upon me by my top rank in the school's hierarchy. Replying before the other girls and being asked to explain a math problem or to read certain passages out loud because I have perfect intonation ensures that I feel quite at home in class. I am not particularly studious or hardworking, handing in hastily-written homework which I rush through in no time. Being naturally talkative and noisy, I delight in playing the part of the bad, unruly pupil, as this will save me from being ostracized by the other girls on account of my good grades.

In 1951-1952, I am in fifth grade with Mademoiselle L, whose reputation as an ogress is well known to all the girls before they reach her class. Back in fourth grade we would hear her shouting and beating the desks with her ruler through the flimsy partition. When we leave school for lunch and at the end of the day, no doubt because of her booming voice, she is assigned to stand there by the front entrance, barking out the names of the young ones sitting on benches in the playground, whose parents are waiting outside. She is short—when term started I was already taller than her—flat-chested, restless, of indefinite age, with a gray chignon, a round face and spectacles with magnifying lenses that make her eyes look enormous. Like the other lay

Sisters, she wears a blue and black striped cape over her smock in winter. If the lesson requires no writing, she makes us sit with our arms crossed behind our backs, heads held high, eyes staring straight ahead. She is forever threatening to send us back to fourth grade and, if we can't solve a math problem, she keeps us in detention until we find the right answer. Only stories about God, saints and martyrs seem to move her, bringing tears to her eyes. The other subjects, spelling, history and arithmetic, are taught without love, with harshness and vehemence; we are expected to toil over them with a view to passing the examination organized in our diocese by the episcopate, echoing the one that grants access to junior high school in the state system. She is feared by parents, who praise her severity, directed against all pupils without exception. The girls are proud of saying that their teacher is the most formidable figure in school, as if it were some torment they silently endure. This doesn't stop us from resorting to the usual tricks to evade her authority: talking with our hand in front of our mouth or behind our raised desk, writing words on an eraser and passing it round and so on. Occasionally her shouts and demands are met by a wave of inertia; although triggered by the slower students, it ultimately spreads to the other girls, the ones eager to please her. She bursts into tears, sitting at her desk, and we must ask to be forgiven, one after the other.

The question of whether or not I liked Mademoiselle L is irrelevant. She was the most educated person I knew. She was a different class of woman, quite unlike my aunts or my mother's customers. She was the living embodiment of authority and could guarantee the excellence of my scholastic being every time I reeled off a poem or handed in a faultless dictation. I always measure myself against her, rather than my classmates: I must know everything she knows by the end of the year. (This was linked to the long-standing belief that teachers knew nothing more than what they taught us; hence the profound respect and fear felt for those who taught "senior classes" and the contempt felt for those whose classes we had left behind and there-fore whom we had surpassed.) When she silences me to give the others a chance to reply or when she tells me to explain the grammatical structure of a sentence, I become her ally. In my mind, her determination to hunt down the slightest of my academic failings is a means of elevating me into her own world of perfection. One day she criticized the way I wrote the letter "m," the first down stroke slight-ly curved on the inside, like an elephant's trunk, snicker-ing, "*it looks dirty.*" I said nothing but blushed. I knew what she meant and she knew that I knew: "You do your 'ms' like a man's penis."

That summer I sent her a postcard from Lourdes.

(As I describe my educational background in 1952, the Communion photograph is gradually becoming more familiar. The solemn face, the unblinking gaze, the faint smile, proud rather than wistful—these features are growing less blurred. The "text" brings the picture into focus, in the same way that the photograph illustrates my writing. Now I can see the good little girl who goes to private school, enjoying the power and ideology of a world symbolizing truth, progress and perfection, a world which, in her eyes, she would never fail.)

(I can now "visualize" the classroom from the seat I was assigned in late December or thereabouts: I sat in the first row on the left—starting from Mademoiselle L's desk—alone at a bench made for two, next to its twin, occupied by Brigitte D, her domed forehead hidden by thick black wavy hair. Turning round, sideways, I can picture the rest of the classroom: light areas with figures vaguely moving around, dressed in different smocks, faces with many sharp details—their hairstyle, their lips (Françoise H's were chapped, Eliane L's flabby), their complexion (Denise R had freckles)—without being able to capture the whole scene. I can hear their voices and a few sentences I have come to associate with them, often quite incongruous: "Can you speak Javanese?" Simone D wants to know. There are also dark areas where I can identify no one because I have forgotten the names.)

There were other classifications that mattered besides my report card, the kind that eventually develop within any close-knit community, conveyed by "I like" or "I don't like" so-and-so. First a distinction was to be made between the "show-offs" and the others, between the girls who "gave themselves airs" because they got asked to dance at parties or spent their summer vacation by the sea, and those who didn't. Being a show-off is a physical and social trait belonging to the younger, prettier girls from the town center, whose parents are usually traveling salesmen or storekeepers. Among those who aren't show-offs are the daughters of farmers; these older girls, many of whom are repeating their grade, are either boarders or else day students who cycle over from some nearby village. The things they could boast about—the land, the harvesters, the farm hands—fail to make an impression, like anything else to do with the country. Anything associated with "the sticks" is held in contempt. "This ain't no farmhouse!" is an insult.

Another classification that haunts me from October to June is the gradual metamorphosis of the girls' bodies which, until then, were all childishly innocent. There are the little girls, with skinny thighs and short skirts, ribbons and clips in their hair, and the big girls sitting at the back of the classroom, often the older ones. I watch out for changes in their physical appearance and dress—a blouse billowing out, nylon stockings for going out on Sunday. I try hard to make out a sanitary pad underneath their dress. It is their company I seek in order to learn about sexual matters. In a world where neither parents nor teachers refer to what is obviously a mortal sin, a world where one is continually spying on adult conversation to glimpse snatches of the secret, only the older girls can pass on information. Their very bodies have become a silent source of knowledge. Who was it who said to me, "if you were a boarder, we'd go to the dorm and I'd show you my sanitary napkin full of blood."

The image of a young girl suggested by the photograph taken in Biarritz is deceptive. In Mademoiselle L's class, although I am among the tallest, I am flat-chested and show no signs of puberty. That year I am anxious to start having my period. Every time I see a new girl, I wonder if she has started to menstruate. I feel inferior because I haven't started my period yet. In fifth grade, I resented these physical disparities more than anything else.

I did everything I could to look older. If it hadn't been forbidden by my mother and condemned by the private school, I would have gone to church in stockings and high heels, with painted lips, at the age of eleven and a half. My permed hair was the only touch of sophistication I was allowed. In spring 1952, for the first time, my mother agreed to let me have two dresses with knife pleats that hugged my hips and a pair of shoes with wedge heels, barely a few centimeters high. She said no to the wide, black stretch belt which fastened with two metal clips and which accentuated the waistline and buttocks of many girls and women that summer. I remember how I longed for that belt and how much I missed not having it all summer.

(Drawing up a rapid inventory of the year 1952, as well as the images I have, I can remember the songs *Ma p'tite folie* and *Mexico*, the black stretch belt, my mother's blue crepe dress, the one with red and yellow flowers, and a manicure set in black plastic—as if only material objects could account for the passing of time. The clothes, advertisements, songs and movies that come and go over a year or even a single season help us re-arrange our feelings and desires into some kind of chronological order. To be sure, the black stretch belt marks the awakening of my desire to seduce men, of which I can find no trace before, just like the song *Miami Beach Rhumba* reflects my yearning for romance and faraway lands. In his writings, Proust suggests that our memory is separate from us, residing in the ocean breeze or the smells of early autumn—things linked to the earth that recur periodically, confirming the permanence of mankind. For me and no doubt many of my contemporaries, memories are associated with ephemeral things such as a fashionable belt or a summer hit and therefore the act of remembering can do nothing to reaffirm my sense of identity or continuity. It can only confirm the fragmented nature of my life and the belief that I belong to history.)

Somewhere above the class, forming an inaccessible group, were the "senior girls"—the name used by the staff to designate students attending high school, from sixth grade to twelfth grade. The senior of these senior girls would switch classrooms between lessons and we could see them walking down the corridors with bulging briefcases. They made no noise in class and never played, conversing in small groups, standing under the lime trees or leaning against the chapel wall. I seem to recall that we spent all our time watching them and that they never even glanced at us. They were a model for us, an image to which we aspired both inside and outside of school. Because of their pubescent bodies and especially their knowledge—vast and mysterious, ranging from Latin to algebra, glimpsed on prize-giving day—I was convinced that they could feel only contempt for us. Having to enter a ninth grade classroom with a confession note filled me with terror. I could feel their eyes staring at the pathetic fifth grade pupil who had dared interrupt the imperial process of learning. After I had left the room, I was surprised not to have been greeted by a deafening chorus of sniggers and catcalls. I had no idea that some of the older girls were struggling to keep up, repeating the grade once or in some cases twice. And assuming I had known it, I would still have thought them superior: even those girls knew a lot more than I did.

That year, before afternoon class resumed, I would look out for one of the senior girls in seventh grade, searching for her in the playground lineup. She was frail, with a narrow waist, shoulder-length curly black hair masking her forehead and ears, a round face, soft and milky. I may have noticed her because we had the same red leather zip-up bootees when the fashion was to wear black rubber snow boots. It never occurred to me that she might notice me or speak to me. I enjoyed studying her—her hair, her bare, rounded calves—and overhearing her conversation. All I wanted to know was her first name and the street she lived in: Françoise Renout or Renault, route du Havre.

As far as I can recall, I didn't have any friends at school. I never visited any of the other girls and none of them came to my home. Besides, we just didn't meet outside of school, except when we shared the same route. Traveling to and from school was the only opportunity we had to form friendships. I walked part of the way with Monique B, the daughter of a local farmer; in the morning she would leave her bicycle with her aging aunt, with whom she would also have lunch, and would pick it up in the evening. Tall and flat-chested like me, she had chubby cheeks and thick lips, with traces of food around the edges. She worked desperately hard to achieve mediocre results. When I went round to her aunt's house to pick her up at one o' clock, we would start by telling each other what we had just eaten.

As I was the only girl in the family and the neighborhood to have a private education, there was no one, apart from my classmates, with whom to share my school secrets.

(I remember a game I used to play in the morning on the days when I didn't have school and would lie in until midday. On the back of a blank postcard—an elderly woman had given me a whole pile of old ones—I write down the surname and Christian name of a girl. No address, just the name of the town pictured on the card. No text in the part set aside for correspondence. The surnames and Christian names are provided by newspapers such as *Lisette*, *Le Petit Écho de la mode* and *Les Veillées des chaumières*. I make a point of using the chronological order in which they were published. Then I cross out some of the names to add new ones and prolong the game. Inventing dozens of addressees gives me intense satisfaction (something akin to sexual desire). Occasionally, not very often, I send myself a card, blank, just like the other ones.)

People say of me, *school is everything for her*.

My mother relays the religious code and the principles dictated by my school. She goes to Mass several times a week, attends vespers in winter, the Benediction of the Holy Sacrament, the Lenten sermon and the Stations of the Cross on Good Friday. Since her youth, processions and other religious celebrations have always provided her with a legitimate excuse for getting dressed up and being seen in respectable company. She included me in these festivities from an early age (memories of a long walk in search of the statue of Our Lady of Boulogne along the route du Havre) and would promise to treat me to a procession or a visit to Notre-Dame-de-Bonsecours Cathedral as though it were a Sunday picnic in the forest. When there are no customers, in the afternoon, she goes upstairs and kneels at the foot of her bed, before the crucifix hanging just above. In the bedroom I share with my parents are three framed pictures: a huge photograph of Sainte Thérèse de Lisieux, a reproduction of the Holy Face and an engraving of Sacré-Cœur Cathedral; on the mantelpiece, two statues portraying the Virgin, one made of alabaster, the other one coated in a sort of orangey paint that glows in the dark. In the evening, from our respective beds, my mother and I take turns to recite the morning prayers we say in class. We eat no meat, whether steak or sausages, on Fridays. A one-day bus trip to Lisieux—Mass and Communion at the Carmelite chapel, guided tour of the basilica and Les Buissonnets, the house where Sainte Thérèse was born—is the only important summer outing for the whole family.

Just after the war, my mother took part in the pilgrimage to Lourdes organized by our diocese, to attend a thanksgiving service for the Virgin Mary, who had watched over us during the bombings.

For my mother, religion is seen as something *noble*, to be bracketed with knowledge, culture and a good education. Failing proper instruction, self-advancement starts with going to Mass and listening to the priest's sermon; it's a way of *opening up one's mind*. She doesn't always go along with the principles and objectives of the private school, dismissing their ban on books (she buys and reads a great many novels and newspapers, which she passes on to me) and ignoring their call for obedience and self-sacrifice, thought to be detrimental to a successful career. She is wary of the missionary zeal shown by the "Croisées" and other Roman Catholic organizations: a surfeit of religious instruction impinges on spelling and arithmetic. Religion must remain an auxiliary to education, it must never take its place. If I decided to take the veil, it would displease her, ruining all her hopes.

Converting the rest of the world does not interest her or maybe she thinks it inappropriate in the case of a storekeeper—just a friendly remark to the local girls who have deserted Mass. My mother's religion, shaped by her experience in the factory and molded by her fierce, ambitious personality and her work, can be summed up as:

—a highly individualistic approach, a way of seizing every opportunity to ensure material comfort

—a distinguishing feature that sets her aside from the rest of the family and most of the customers from our neighborhood

—a social ambition, showing the snooty bourgeois women from downtown that her religious fervor and generous donations in church have made her a better person

—the cornerstone of her universal quest for perfection and self-improvement, which embraces my own future.

(I find it difficult to convey the full extent to which religion governed my mother's life. In 1952, for me, my mother *was* religion. She appropriated the rules of private education, only she made them harsher. Among her favorite recommendations: *take the example of* (their kind, polite behavior, their diligence) but *don't try to copy* (their failings). She was always saying, *be an example* (by working hard, behaving properly, being polite). And, *what will people think?*)

The newspapers and novels she passes on to me, along with the *Bibliothèque verte* books, do not contradict the principles of private education. They all satisfy the prerequisite for authorized reading, which is *to be safely read by all*: *Les Veillées des chaumières*, *Le Petit Écho de la mode*, and novels by Delly and Max du Veuzit. Some books carry a stamp on their cover—"Distinguished by the French Academy"— confirming their compliance with moral standards rather than their literary value. In my twelfth year, I already have the first volumes of the *Brigitte* collection by Berthe Bernage, which features fifteen titles in all. Presented in the form of a diary, they recount the life story of Brigitte— betrothed, married, mother and grandmother. I shall have the whole collection by the time I'm seventeen. In the foreword to *Brigitte jeune fille*, the author writes:

Although Brigitte has doubts and errs she always reverts to the straight and narrow (...) because the story wants to be true to life. A soul of noble stock, an elevated soul, strengthened by fine examples, wise lessons, a healthy family background and Christian discipline, that soul may be exposed to the temptation of "living like everybody else" and sacrificing his or her sense of duty to pleasure but ultimately duty will prevail whatever the price.... A worthy French woman will always be a woman who loves her family and her country. And who seeks solace in prayer.

Brigitte embodies the model young girl, humble and contemptuous of creature comforts, living in a world where people have drawing-rooms and pianos, frequent tennis courts, visit art shows and sip afternoon tea in the Bois de Boulogne. A world where parents never argue. The book conveys the excellence of Christian moral standards, as well as the excellence of the bourgeois way of life.*

(I found these stories more realistic than Dickens' novels because they painted the picture of a likely future—love-marriage-children. Can the real therefore be defined as a mere sum of potentialities?

When I was reading *Brigitte jeune fille* and *Esclave ou reine* by Delly, and going to see the movie *Pas si bête* starring Bourvil, at the same time other people were buying *Saint Genet* by Sartre, *Requiem des innocents* by Calaferte and going to see Ionesco's *The Chairs* on stage. For me these two categories will always remain distinct.)

My father will only read the local newspaper; he never mentions religion except to bark at my mother—"you spend all day in church," "I can't think what you find to say, chattering to the priest all day"—or to crack jokes about the celibacy of clergymen, which she never acknowledges, conveying that such obscenities are beneath her. He attends half the

---

* By the year 2050 magazines like *Cosmopolitan* and *Elle* and the many novels in which society offers a moral code of conduct will of course seem as strange as *Brigitte* does today.

Sunday service, standing at the back of the church to slip away more easily, and waits until Low Sunday—the last limit before transgressing Church rules and committing a mortal sin—to grudgingly make his Easter duty (making confession and taking Holy Communion). My mother expects nothing more from him than this bare minimum, which will ensure the salvation of his spirit. In the evening he doesn't join in our prayers, pretending to be already asleep. Because he shows none of the signs of genuine religious faith and therefore the ambition to *better himself*, my father is not the one to *lay down the law*.

Yet for him, like for my mother, private education is the supreme reference: "What would they say at school, if they could see you now, if they could hear the way you talk," and so on.

And especially, *you mustn't get a bad name at school.*

I have brought to light the codes and conventions of the circles in which I lived. I have listed the different languages that enveloped me, forging the vision I had of myself and the outside world. Nowhere could I fit in that Sunday in June.

What happened that day could not be put into words, in either of the worlds that was mine.

We stopped being decent people, the sort who don't drink or fight and who dress properly to go into town. Despite a brand-new smock to start the term, my beautiful missal, my top grades and my daily prayers, I would never be like the other girls again. I had seen the unseeable. I knew something that the Catholic school and its sheltered environment should have guarded me against, something that implicitly bracketed me with those whose violent, alcoholic nature and mental illness gave rise to stories ending in "really, it's a disgrace to see that."

I became unworthy of private education, its standards of excellence and perfection. I began living in shame.

The worst thing about shame is that we imagine we are the only ones to experience it.

I was still in a state of shock when I took the entrance examination organized by our diocese, receiving a 70% pass, to the surprise and disappointment of Mademoiselle L. It was on the following Wednesday—June 18.

The Sunday after that, on June 22, I attended the gathering organized in Rouen by the Christian Youth Movement, like I had done the year before. The pupils were driven back by bus late at night. Mademoiselle L was in charge of seeing the girls back home in an area that included my neighborhood. It was around one o' clock in the morning. I knocked on the shutters pinned over the grocery door. After some time, the lights went on in the store and my mother appeared in the glare of the doorway, disheveled, silent and sleepy-eyed, in a nightgown that was both creased and soiled (we would use the garment to wipe ourselves after peeing). Mademoiselle L and the girls, two or three of them, immediately stopped talking. My mother mumbled good evening, to which no one replied. I rushed into the store to stop it all. It was the first time I saw my mother through the eyes of the private school. In my memory, this scene, although barely comparable to the one in which my father tried to kill my mother, is seen as its sequel. As if the sight of my mother's loose, unsupported flesh and suspect nightgown had exposed the way we lived and who we truly were.

(Naturally, it never occurred to me that if my mother had owned a bathrobe and had slipped it on over her nightgown, the girls and the teacher from my private school would not have been seized with dismay and I would have no recollection of that particular evening. In our world bathrobes and dressing gowns were considered luxuries; women who dressed for work as soon as they got up had no use for such incongruous, absurd garments. In my system of thinking, which ruled out the existence of bathrobes, it was impossible to escape shame.)

I feel that all the events of that summer served only to confirm our state of disgrace: "no one except us" behaves this way.

My grandmother succumbed to a pulmonary embolism at the beginning of July. I wasn't affected by her death. About ten days later, in the Corderie neighborhood, a violent dispute broke out between one of my cousins, recently married, and his aunt, my mother's sister, the one who lived in my grandmother's house. In the middle of the street, in full view of the neighbors, egged on by his father my uncle Joseph, who was sitting on the embankment, my cousin proceeded to beat his aunt black and blue. Bruised all over and covered in blood, she rushed into the store. My mother accompanied her to the police station and took her to see the doctor. (The incident was tried in court a few months later.)

I contracted a cold and a bad cough which stayed with me all month. Then quite suddenly my right ear got blocked. It wasn't customary to have the doctor come round for a cold in summer. I couldn't hear my own voice and other people's voices sounded muffled. I avoided speaking. I thought I would have to live like this for the rest of my life.

Another incident, also in July, shortly before or after the argument in the rue de la Corderie. One evening, after the café had closed, while we were sitting having dinner, I kept complaining that the frames of my spectacles were crooked.

While I was fiddling with them, my mother suddenly grabbed them and, screaming, hurled them on to the kitchen floor. The lenses shattered into tiny pieces. All I can remember is a loud clamor—my parents flinging insults at each other and my own sobs. I felt that some terrible tragedy had to follow its course, something like, "now we really are living in madness."

This can be said about shame: those who experience it feel that anything can happen to them, that the shame will never cease and that it will only be followed by more shame.

Some time after my grandmother's death and the injuries sustained by my aunt, I went on a bus trip to Étretat with my mother—our traditional one-day summer outing to the seaside. She traveled there and back in her mourning clothes, waiting until she got to the beach to slip on her blue crepe dress, the one with red and yellow flowers, "to stop people in Y from gossiping." A photograph she took of me, mislaid or deliberately thrown away twenty years ago, showed me standing in the sea with water up to my knees, with the Aiguille and the Aval cliff top pictured in the background. I am holding myself perfectly straight, my arms hanging down my sides, trying to pull in my stomach and push out my non-existent breasts, squeezed into a knitted woolen swimsuit.

That winter my mother signed my father and myself up for a package tour organized by the local bus operator. The idea was to go to Lourdes, visiting a few tourist spots on the way down (Rocamadour, the Padirac chasm), to stay there for three or four days and to head back toward Normandy by a different route, via Biarritz, Bordeaux and the *châteaux* of the Loire. My mother had already been to Lourdes on her own—now it was our turn to go. The morning we left, during the second half of August—it was still dark—we stood for ages on the sidewalk of the rue de la République, waiting for the bus that was coming from a small coastal town where it had to pick up some passengers. We drove all day, pausing at a café in Dreux in the morning and stopping for lunch at a restaurant in Olivet, along the banks of the Loiret river. In the afternoon rain set in and I could no longer make out the landscape through the window. I had grazed my finger in the café in Dreux, breaking a lump of sugar into two to give to a dog, and now it was beginning to go septic. As we were heading south, I began to feel disorientated by the change of scenery. I feared that I might never see my mother again. Apart from a crackers manufacturer and his wife, there was no one we knew. It was night-time when we reached Limoges and checked into the Hôtel

Moderne. For dinner, we sat alone at a table in the middle of the dining hall. We dared not speak because of the waiters. We felt intimidated and vaguely apprehensive.

Right from the beginning, people kept the same seat and stayed there throughout the trip (making it easy for me to remember them). In the front row on the right, just ahead of us, were two young girls from Y, belonging to a family of jewelers. Behind us sat a widow, who owned some land, and her thirteen-year-old daughter, enrolled at a convent school in Rouen. In the next row there was a retired post office clerk—a widow, also from Rouen. Further on, a schoolmistress working for state education, unmarried, overweight, in a chocolate brown coat and sandals. In the front row on the left was the crackers manufacturer with his wife; behind them, a couple from the small coastal town, who sold cloth and ladies' fashion wear, the young wives of the two bus drivers and three farming couples. It was the first time we were in the situation of having to spend ten days in the company of complete strangers, all of whom were better off than us, with the exception of the bus drivers.

The next few days, I wasn't quite so upset by being away from home. I enjoyed discovering the mountains and the hot weather—inconceivable in Normandy—eating out twice a day and sleeping in hotels. Being able to wash in a basin, with hot and cold running water, was a luxury for me.

I thought that it was "nicer at the hotel than back at home"—something I always felt while I was living with my parents, proof maybe that I belonged to the world down below. Every time we checked into a hotel, I was anxious to see my new bedroom. I could have stayed there for hours, doing nothing, just being there.

My father continued to be wary of everything we saw. During the bus trip, he kept watching the road, which was often quite steep, and paid more attention to the driver's conduct than to the landscape. He resented having to sleep in a different bed every night. Food was particularly important to him: he was suspicious of the dishes we were served, which we had never tasted before, and was critical of ordinary produce, like bread or potatoes, which he grew in his garden. When we visited churches and *châteaux*, he would lag behind, visibly bored, as if he was only doing it to please me. He was not in his element, in other words, not doing things and seeing people that reflected his usual tastes and lifestyle.

He began loosening up when he made friends with the retired post office clerk, the crackers manufacturer and the cloth merchant, who were more talkative than the other passengers because of their job and who shared some of his concerns (corporate taxes) despite the obvious differences between them—they all had scrubbed hands. They were all older than my father and, like him, had no intention of traipsing around in the sun all day. Therefore they spent plenty of time over meals. Conversation touched on the arid landscapes we had driven through, the recent drought, the Mediterranean accent, anything that was different from where we lived, and the Lurs murder case.

I had thought it the normal thing to do to seek the company of thirteen-year-old Élisabeth: after all, there was only one year between us and she too went to convent school, even if she was already in seventh grade. We were the same height but her blouse billowed out and she looked like a young girl already. On the first day, I was glad to see that we were both wearing a navy blue pleated skirt and a jacket; hers was red, mine was orange. She did not acknowledge my advances; when I spoke to her she would just smile, looking very much like her mother, whose mouth opened on to several gold teeth and who never said a word to my father. One day I put on my gym outfit—a blouse and skirt—which we had to wear out now that the Christian Youth gathering was over. It did not escape her attention: "You too went to the fair?" I was proud to say yes, mistaking her question and beaming smile for a sign of intimacy between us. Then, catching her strange intonation, I realized that it meant, "so you've got nothing else to wear except your gym suit."

One day I caught these words, uttered by a woman traveling in our group, "she'll be a real beauty later on." Afterward I realized that it wasn't me she was talking about but Élisabeth.

There was no question of my approaching the two girls from the jewelry store. I had no place among the women's bodies traveling on the bus; I was just a child growing up— tall, flat and healthy-looking.

When we arrived in Lourdes, I succumbed to a strange condition. Everything I saw—the houses, the mountains, the entire landscape—kept filing by in front of me. When I was sitting in the hotel restaurant, the outside wall opposite kept whizzing past my eyes. It was only indoors that things stayed still. I didn't say anything to my father; I thought that I had gone mad and that this condition would stay with me all my life. Every morning, when I got up, I wondered if the landscape had stopped spinning. I seem to remember that things were back to normal by the time we reached Biarritz.

My father and I duly performed the devotions recommended by my mother. Taking part in the torchlit procession, attending High Mass out in the open, under the beating sun—a woman lent me her folding chair when I almost passed out—saying our prayers in the Grotto of the Miracles. I could not say whether I enjoyed visiting these places, which caused my mother and schoolmistresses to go into raptures. I felt nothing while I was there. I recall being vaguely bored, on a gray misty morning, somewhere along the banks of the Gave river.

Along with the group, we visited the medieval castle, the caves at Bétharram and the Panorama, a sort of tent with a huge circular screen inside reproducing the landscape in the days of Bernadette Soubirous. Apart from the retired post office employee, we were the only ones not to visit the Gavarnie cirque and the Spanish bridge. These excursions weren't included in the package tour and my father probably hadn't taken enough money with him. (At a sidewalk café in Biarritz, he is dismayed to hear the price of the Cognacs he and the other two tradesmen have been drinking.)

Neither of us had formed any preconceived idea about the trip. There were so many customs we knew nothing about.

The young girls from the jewelry store had a guidebook which they could be seen holding every time they left the bus to visit a monument. They rummaged in their beach bag and brought out cookies and chocolate. Except for a bottle of mentholated spirit and a few sugar lumps, in case we felt sick, we had brought no food with us, thinking it improper to do so.

I had only one pair of shoes, white, bought for the Communion ceremony, and they soon became grubby. My mother hadn't given me any white polish. It never occurred to us to go out and buy some; that seemed impossible in a strange town, where we didn't know any of the stores.... One evening, in Lourdes, seeing all the pairs of shoes lined up outside the bedroom doors, I decided to put mine down too. The next morning they were no cleaner and my father teased me: "I told you so. You have to pay for that." This was not something that was conceivable for us.

All we bought were medals and a few postcards to send to my mother, the family and the people we knew. No newspapers, except *Le Canard enchaîné*, just once. The places we drove through gave no news of our area in the local press.

In Biarritz, I had no swimsuit or shorts. We are walking along the beach, fully dressed among the suntanned bodies in their bikinis.

Again, Biarritz: sitting outside a big café, my father embarks on a dirty story about a priest which I have already heard back home. The others give a forced laugh.

Three images, on the way back.

During a stop on a sandy plateau with burnt vegetation, possibly in the Auvergne. I have just finished defecating far from the group, who are sitting at a roadside café. I realize that I have left part of myself in a place where I shall probably never come back. In a few hours, tomorrow, I shall be far away, back at school, yet this part of me will remain abandoned on this barren plateau for days and days, until winter.

Standing on the staircase in the *château* of Blois. My father, who has caught a cold, is seized with a fit of coughing. All you can hear is his cough, echoing under the vaults, drowning out the guide's commentary. He waits behind while the other members of the group reach the top of the staircase. I turn round and wait for him, possibly with some reluctance.

One evening—it was our last day—in Tours, we had dinner in a brightly-lit restaurant where the walls were lined with mirrors, frequented by a sophisticated clientele. My father and I were seated at the end of a long table set up for the group. The waiters were paying little attention to us; we had to wait a long time between courses. At a small table nearby sat a girl aged fourteen or fifteen, suntanned, in a low-cut dress, and an elderly man who appeared to be her father.

They were talking and laughing quite freely, completely at ease, oblivious of other people. She was dipping into a thick milky substance in a glass—some years later I learnt this was yogurt, which people like us had never heard of. I caught sight of myself in the mirror, pale and sad-looking with my spectacles, silently sitting beside my father, who was staring into the far distance. I could see everything that separated me from that girl yet I wouldn't have known what to do to resemble her.

Afterward, my father complained with unusual vehemence about this restaurant, where he claimed we had been served mashed potatoes made with "pig slop," white and tasteless. Several weeks later, he was still venting his anger over the meal and its disgraceful "pig slop." Although he never actually said so—it was probably then that I began decoding his speech—it was his way of expressing resentment at having been treated with contempt because we were not chic customers who ate "*à la carte*."

(After evoking the images I have of that summer, I feel inclined to write "then I discovered that" or "then I realized that," words implying a clear perception of the events one has lived through. But in my case there is no understanding, only this feeling of shame that has fossilized the images and stripped them of meaning. The fact that I experienced such inertia and nothingness is something that cannot be denied. It is the ultimate truth.

It is the bond between the little girl of 1952 and the woman who is writing this manuscript.

Except for Bordeaux, Tours and Limoges, I never went back to any of the places we visited during that trip.

The restaurant scene in Tours is by far the most vivid. When I was writing a book about my father's life and roots, it would haunt me relentlessly, proof that there existed two separate worlds and that we would always belong to the one down below.

Chronology may be the only connection between the scene of that Sunday in June and the bus trip to Lourdes. Yet who can say that an incident following in the wake of another is not somehow overshadowed by the first one? And who can say that the natural order of events does not carry meaning?)

After we had got back home, I couldn't stop thinking about our trip. I kept seeing myself in hotel rooms and restaurants, or walking down sun-drenched avenues. Now I knew there was another world—a huge place with a blazing sun, bedrooms and washbasins with hot water, and little girls talking to their father the way they do in novels. We were not part of it. That's the way it was.

I'm pretty sure it was that summer that I invented the "perfect day" game, a sort of ritual inspired by *Le Petit Écho de la mode*—which boasted far more advertisements than the other papers we bought—after I had read through the serials and a few of the articles. The game always went the same way. I would imagine I was a young girl living alone in a big, beautiful house (alternatively, living alone in a room in Paris). I would shape my body and appearance using the products advertised in the magazine: pretty teeth (Gibbs), luscious red lips (Rouge Baiser), a slender figure (girdle X) and so on. I would usually be wearing a dress or a suit available by mail order; my furniture would come from the department store Les Galeries Barbès. The academic studies I chose were those which the École Universelle claimed provided the best job opportunities. I wouldn't eat food unless its nutritional value was stated: pasta, Astra margarine. I would delight in forging my personality out of the products advertised only in that particular paper (a rule scrupulously observed), slowly taking time to explore each new "ad," piecing the images together to paint the picture of a perfect day. One possible scenario would involve waking up in a

Lévitan bed, having a bowl of Banania for breakfast, brushing my "glossy hair" with Vitapointe and studying my correspondence course to become a nurse or maybe a social worker. Every week a new batch of advertisements would rekindle the game which, unlike the fantasies derived from literature, was both creative and exciting—I was using real objects to build the future—as well as frustrating—I could never work out a schedule for the whole day.

It was a secret, nameless activity which, in my mind, could not possibly be shared by others.

In September business suddenly grew slack: a Coop or Familistère store had opened in the town center. The trip to Lourdes had no doubt proved too heavy a burden financially. In the afternoon, my parents would talk in low voices in the kitchen. One day my mother accused my father and myself of not having prayed properly in the grotto at Lourdes. We burst out laughing and she blushed, as if she had revealed a secret bond she shared with heaven, which was beyond our understanding. They were thinking of selling the business and getting taken on as store assistants in a grocery, or else going back to the factory. The situation must have taken a turn for the better because none of that happened.

Toward the end of the month, a decayed tooth was giving me trouble so for the first time in my life my mother took me to see the dentist in Y. Before releasing a jet of cold water on to my gum for the injection, he asked me: "Does it hurt when you drink cider?" It was the usual drink among workers and country people, both adults and children. At home I would drink water, like the girls from my school, occasionally adding a few drops of grenadine. (Was I doomed to pick up every single sentence that reminded us of our place in society?)

At the beginning of the school term, a group of two or three of us were busy cleaning the classroom one Saturday afternoon in the company of Madame B, the teacher in charge of the sixth grade. Carried away by my dusting, I broke into the love song *Boléro* at the top of my voice, then immediately stopped. I refused to continue, despite strong encouragement on the part of Madame B, convinced that she would pounce on the first signs of vulgarity I showed before denouncing them violently to the other girls.

There is no point in going on. My shame was followed by more shame, only to be followed by more shame.

Now everything in our life is synonymous with shame—the urinal in the courtyard, the shared bedroom (owing to a common rural practice and the lack of space, I slept in my parents' bed), my mother's violent behavior and crude language, the drunken customers and the families who couldn't pay up. Being acquainted with the various degrees of drunkenness and having to finish off the month with corned beef were enough to put me into a category for which those at private school felt only indifference and scorn.

It was normal to feel ashamed: I saw it as an inescapable fatality resulting from my parents' occupation, their financial troubles, their working-class background and the way we generally behaved. And the events of that Sunday in June. Shame became a new way of living for me. I don't think I was even aware of it, it had become part of my own body.

I have always wanted to write the sort of book that I find it impossible to talk about afterward, the sort of book that makes it impossible for me to withstand the gaze of others. But what degree of shame could possibly be conveyed by the writing of a book which seeks to measure up to the events I experienced in my twelfth year.

Summer 1996 is drawing to an end. When I began thinking about this text, the market square in Sarajevo suffered a mortar attack that killed several dozen people and wounded hundreds of others. In the written press some journalists wrote, "we are overcome by shame." For them, shame was something they could feel one day and not the next, something that applied to one situation (Bosnia) and not another (Rwanda). No one remembers the blood shed on the market place in Sarajevo.

While I was writing this book, my attention was immediately caught by any news item, however slight, attributed to the year 1952—the release of a movie, the publication of a book, the death of an artist and so on. I felt that these events brought home the reality of that faraway year and my identity as a child. In his novel *Fires on the Plain*, published in 1952, the Japanese author Shohei Ooka writes: "All this may just be an illusion but all the same I cannot question the things I have experienced. Memories too belong in that category."

I look at the picture taken in Biarritz. My father has been dead for twenty-nine years. The only link between me and the little girl in the photograph is what happened that Sunday in June, a scene which she carries around in her head and which prompted me to write this book because it is still with me today. Only this can bring the two of us together since orgasm, the moment when my sense of identity and coherence is at its highest, was something that I was not to experience until two years later.

October 1996

ALSO BY ANNIE ERNAUX

CLEANED OUT

EXTERIORS

A FROZEN WOMAN

"I REMAIN IN DARKNESS"

A MAN'S PLACE

SIMPLE PASSION

A WOMAN'S STORY